The Dog
who Loved
the Moon

To Camille, who loves to dance
—C. G.

For Marta and Sira, who love dancing
—S. S.

Atheneum Books for Young Readers
An imprint of Simon & Schuster Children's Publishing Division
1230 Avenue of the Americas, New York, New York 10020
Text copyright © 2008 by Cristina García
Illustrations copyright © 2008 by Sebastià Serra
Book design by Debra Sfetsios
The text for this book is set in Formata.
The illustrations for this book are rendered digitally.
Manufactured in China
First Edition
10 9 8 7 6 5 4 3 2 1
Library of Congress Cataloging-in-Publication Data
García, Cristina, 1958–
The dog who loved the moon / Cristina García ; illustrated by Sebastià Serra. —
1st ed.
p. cm.
Summary: When her dog becomes lovesick for the moon, a young Cuban
girl and her uncle call the moon down to give the dog a kiss, with surprising
results.
ISBN-13: 978-1-4169-1836-3
ISBN-10: 1-4169-1836-1
[1. Dogs—Fiction. 2. Moon—Fiction. 3. Uncles—Fiction. 4. Cuba—Fiction.] I. Serra,
Sebastià, 1966– ill. II. Title.
PZ7.G155624Do 2008
[E]—dc22
2007006428

written by **Cristina García**

The Dog Who Loved the Moon

illustrated by **Sebastià Serra**

Atheneum Books for Young Readers
New York   London   Toronto   Sydney

Pilar received two gifts for her birthday: a pair of pink dancing slippers and a little white puppy. The *zapatillas* she wore every day and every night, even to bed. She needed them in case she had to dance in her dreams. The little white dog she named Paco, after her favorite *tío*, the one who played the conga drums and always had beautiful girlfriends who wore shiny dresses and chewed bubble gum.

Pilar's uncle found *el perrito* one night, wandering by himself under a full moon. Where was his *mami*? Nobody knew.

Paco had a round face and pointy ears and a tail that wagged extra hard when he was happy. He liked to cuddle with Pilar, and sometimes he found his way into her pink slippers, or ended up wearing one as a silly hat.

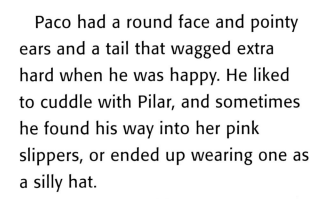

When he ran to greet Pilar after school he always tripped on his too-big paws.

She hugged him hard and together they would share an afternoon snack. They both loved warm *leche* with honey.

Every night Pilar put on music to dance. In her pink dancing slippers, she moved to the beat, stamping and clapping and shaking her hips. She turned, too, fast as a spinning top, but she got so dizzy she had to stop.

"Don't you want to dance?" Pilar asked breathlessly. "It's so much fun!"

But Paco only rested his head on his paws, sighing and scratching, and looked out the window at the sliver of the moon.

As the days grew longer, Pilar's mother decided to throw a *fiesta* to greet the summer sun with music, dancing, and a fresh-baked pineapple cake.

Tío Paco came over with his latest girlfriend, Chachi, who wore a sparkly gown that made her look like a goldfish. Pilar's uncle played the conga drums and everyone sang:

Ay, ay, ay, ay! Como nos caliente el sol!

Pilar translated the words for Paco, just in case he forgot his Spanish:

Oh, oh, oh, oh!
How the sun warms us all!

But as much as everyone tried to get Paco to join in the fun, he simply sat by the window, looking outside. The moon shone in the sky.

"What's wrong with *el perrito*?" Tío Paco asked.

"I wish I knew!" Pilar cried, very worried about her best friend.

"A dog who doesn't dance?" Tío Paco said. "I've never heard of such a thing!"

"He must be in love," Chachi chimed in.

"In love?" Tío Paco and Mamá asked at the same time. "But with whom?"

The days got shorter and autumn drew near. During the day Paco was an ordinary dog, fetching sticks and balls and playing with the calico cat next door, though that wasn't so ordinary for a dog. But come nighttime, his sadness returned, growing bigger and bigger with every moon.

Pilar gave him biscuits and read him bedtime stories to cheer him up. She played her favorite music and tried to get him to dance. She even put her pink *zapatillas* on his feet—on two of them, anyway—and held his front legs up for a *cha-cha-chá*.

"You'll be my partner!" she announced.

But as soon as she let go, Paco returned to watching the moon.

It wasn't as much fun, Pilar thought, to dance all alone.

On the nights the moon was fat and
yellow and completely full, Paco howled
and howled until the neighbors complained.
Once, the police came and threatened to take
Paco away.

"Hush, Paco. Hush!" Pilar scolded her puppy,
who was practically a full-grown dog by now.

Fall turned into winter and the leaves fell off the trees, swirling madly to the ground in crinkly reds and golds. At night it was cold enough to light the fireplace and watch the flames dance. Pilar tried to imitate them. She leaped into the air with her pink-slippered feet, wiggled the tips of her fingers, and tried to make the same crackling sounds as the burning twigs.

"*A bailar!*" she shouted. "Let's dance!"

But Paco only looked away.

Soon it would be the first day of spring, Pilar's birthday again. Her mother asked her what she wanted as a gift, but Pilar just answered: "I think Paco misses his *mami*, so what I want this year is to give him the moon."

"That's very nice of you, *mi cielo*," Mamá said kindly, kissing Pilar on the cheek. "But the moon belongs to everyone. After all, without the moon, nobody would fall in love."

At her birthday party Pilar wore her pink dancing slippers. Tío Paco came over with Chachi and a brand-new set of conga drums. Mamá told them about Pilar's special wish, pointing to the crescent moon.

"Ay, it's so romantic!" Chachi squealed, pretending to dance with the moon in the living room. "Imagine *la luna* coming to visit us!"

"It can't hurt to try." Tío Paco said. He moved a few chairs aside, rearranged his congas, and opened the windows very wide. In no time at all, he was drumming and singing at the top of his lungs.

BaBaLUUUUU-NA! BaBaLUUUUU-NA!
he shouted at the end of every chorus.
Before long everyone was singing and dancing.

BaBaLUUUUUUU

they shouted, happy and excited with the new song. Paco
howled in just the right places and made everyone laugh.
   But he still didn't dance.

Then something mysterious happened.
The moon, which had been hanging
like a sideways smile right outside their
window, . . . disappeared.

Suddenly the night turned black. Tío Paco
stopped drumming, his mouth opened wide
as the window in surprise. Pilar looked up
at the sky, more curious than frightened. Her
mother and Chachi held each other tight.
Where was the moon?

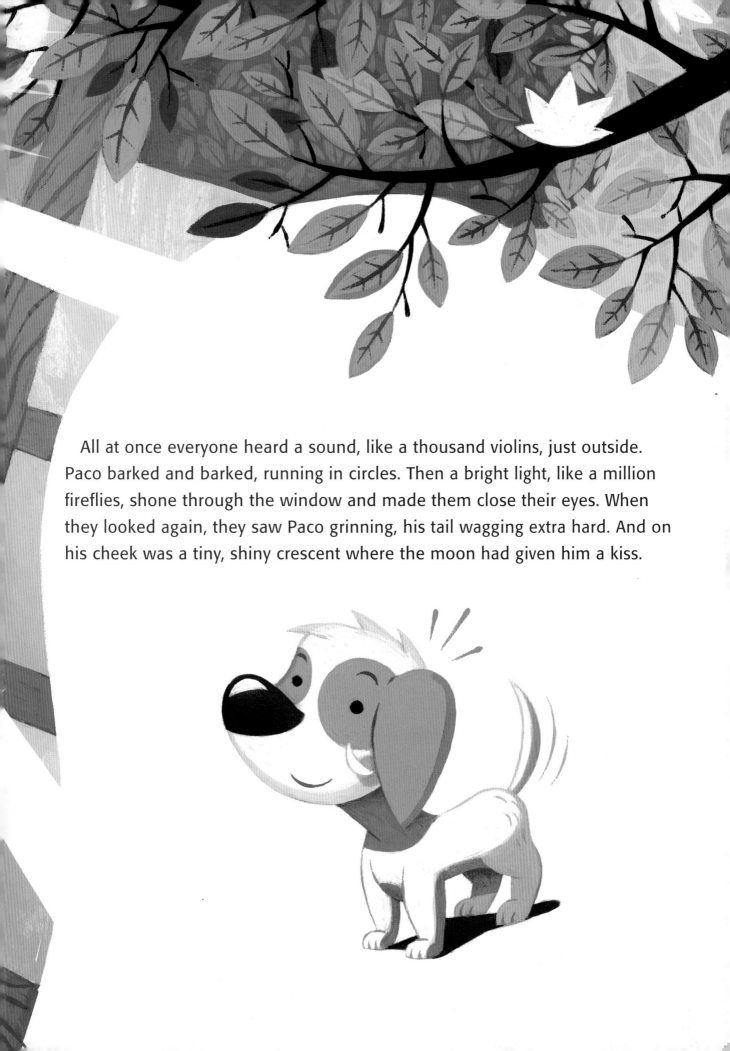

All at once everyone heard a sound, like a thousand violins, just outside. Paco barked and barked, running in circles. Then a bright light, like a million fireflies, shone through the window and made them close their eyes. When they looked again, they saw Paco grinning, his tail wagging extra hard. And on his cheek was a tiny, shiny crescent where the moon had given him a kiss.

Before anyone stopped falling in love, the moon was back where it belonged. The whole family cheered and began their singing and dancing all over again.

BabaLuuuuu-NA!

they roared, shaking their hips.

Only this time Paco joined in, dancing a *cha-cha-chá*
with his very best friend. They twirled and laughed and twirled again
until they were both dizzy with happiness.
And it seemed to Pilar, and to Paco, and to everyone there
that the moon was dancing too.

The End